SANCTUM

A NOVELLA

SANCTUM

ETHAN J. POLLARD

SANCTUM

For a moment as she wakes, the smell—of blood, of offal, of bodies broken open and spilled forth—reminds her not of death but of birth. The scream, the splitting, the violent rending that is the way of all new life. Red miracle, raw as sunrise.

Then she remembers, and the weight of it is barbed and brutal in her chest.

She remains for a time, unmoving against the temple floor, allowing the grief to hold her down and rake her through with bloody claws, groaning cracked and arid in her throat.

After a time, she surfaces, and her body begins to remind her of its treatment. The familiar aches of encroaching age are draped in a stiffening tapestry of new-made pain, the work of fists and swords and the righteous zeal of cruel men.

Images lurch through her mind, smeared flashes of pale faces, demoniac grins. Screams, blood, fear, laughter. Dark and whirling forms, the chunk and spatter of blades into bodies.

A sob snags in her throat like a shard of bone.

Gritting her teeth, she forces it down, forces everything down, crushes it all into a hot, hard knot of granite and bile, lets it fall to lodge somewhere in her belly and burn. There is work to be done now; she will see to it as she always has.

A voice strains at the back of her mind, urgent, clamoring. She rolls, comes slowly to hands and knees. A breath, a moment for the pain to subside. Then she stands. The stones are sticky beneath her feet, a corrupted stench pressing at her nostrils, the back of her throat. Blood in the sun. A faint buzzing whispers from all directions. High on the wall, a single, narrow window permits a thin shaft of sunlight to illumine a section of floor. Dark-stained, glistening.

Everything within her recoils at the thought of moving from where she stands, at beholding what waits beyond this blessedly dim corridor. She swallows behind locked teeth, eyes fluttering closed. Open. She takes a step, bare feet silent on the congealing floor.

Her body twists against her as she moves, flinching away from this lattice of new wounds. Tightness of deepening bruises, the tug and burn of cuts only half-sealed, raw slip of flesh against flesh. New scars in the making, nestling among the old. Blood coats her skin like a pestilence. She feels it drying there, sick and clinging. Unclean. Death-blood.

The sanctuary is littered with broken forms, coated in gore and flies. The day's heat has not been kind. The reek of rotting blood assails her and her knees turn to water, bear her to the floor. Breath thickening, she looks away, up to the great chamber's vaulted ceiling, to the hazy light filtering down like honey. A worthless benediction.

She coughs. Bile floods her mouth, sour and thick on her teeth. She spits it out, stands, steps into the room.

Wind moans through the heights of the chamber, whistling in doorways, raging through the twisted, sun-scoured trees outside. A mourning dirge. A battle-shriek. She breathes slowly, forcing herself forward, body crawling with revulsion, disbelief. They are all here, brothers and sisters of her priesthood, dying where they lived and served and worshiped. Dying alone.

Bitterness surges up in her on another wave of bile, fear crashing behind it. The voice in the back of her mind chatters louder, pushing her on fevered, unsteady legs. She moves between the bodies, eyes dancing away from slit bellies, pooled organs, searching for faces. Searching for one face. Searching—

Here. Broken, naked. Muscled flesh rent in a hundred places. A young man, handsome, tall, broad frame somehow fragile now, smaller with the spirit torn away. Kind, noble, headstrong. Smile brighter than the sun.

His hands curl limply at his sides, blood drying in the cracks.

Grief bears down on her with the weight of worlds. She feels the moment she breaks, a wrenching spasm that moves through her body like a tide, snapping walls and dams and barriers and dashing her to the ground. Her arms wrap the body, clawing him to her, clinging vainly to heavy flesh. A void, an absence. Her voice keens and cracks, animal sounds, haunting the room where the god once dwelt. He does not hear.

In the wake of it, she does not remember how long she worked. Only snatches remain, shredded pieces of memory jutting like bones from a half-buried battlefield: searching the temple for the rest of the bodies, beams of once-holy light falling on scenes of desecration; dragging corpses into rows in the sanctuary, pulling down tapestries to cover them; matching heads to torsos, trying not to see the familiar lines of beloved faces. The high priestess she found broken upon the crystal altar, fine robes ripped away, body hacked and bloody, hair—always an ornate crown, sculpted, perfumed, thick black threaded with gold—now torn, limp, burned.

She gathers them all, lays them in the sanctuary, unaware of the progress of time, if days pass or mere moments. The corrupted aftertaste of violence and lust hangs thick in the air, brushing her with oily fingers wherever she moves. Nothing has been spared. Carvings smashed, furnishings toppled and looted, beds and shrines stained with shit and blood and piss, stinking, cloying. All is defiled. The god has departed.

This is no holy place.

As she performs her grim work, the hot core of rage in her belly cools, hardening into grey steel, filling the hollowed places within her, setting hard between her ribs. Her mouth moves with slow curses, uttered in a language she learned long ago, long before she fled to this place. A powerful tongue—older than mountains, deeper than the night-dark sky. Something twines in her belly. Her mind segments, one half sealing itself away to wall her from grief, the other ticking like a ruthless machine, sifting plans, weighing options. Measured, methodical. Relentless.

She remembers another place, sacred like this one strove to be, but older, much older, and more powerful by far. She remembers the taste of it on her tongue, like blood and honey, heady as liquor. Feels it threading through the iron in her chest, sweet and bitter in her throat. The bite of resolve.

The air is chill in the crystal caverns below the temple, the light dim and cut with colors. She passes the embalmed dead, their peace undisturbed by the carnage above. She does not envy them, but she wishes that she could. So sweet to lie all ignorant in death, wrapped in spices and linen, uncaring. The weight of knowledge lies with the living.

None of the desecrators found this place, it seems. A flicker of bitter relief at that. The secret stores appear untouched, their clasps intact. Opening them, she takes what she needs—clothes, medicine, food, water. A small pouch of coin. The medicine is acrid, the balm hot on her wounds as she rubs it in. She is not hungry, but forces herself to eat. The body is a broken vessel; it must be repaired, made strong for the work ahead.

Grief swells, sudden and vast, overspilling the hastily-made reservoir inside her. She trembles, overcome with an abrupt longing to remain here in this crystal-veined darkness, to crawl down beside the hallowed dead and become like them. A husk, unburdened, unknowing. Weightless as a leaf on the wind.

Instead her body moves, weary but obdurate, independent of her mind. She drops supplies into a pack, removes her torn and bloodied raiment, dresses herself in traveling clothes. Stitched leathers, rough sand-cloak, headscarf, boots. Old but serviceable. Her hand brushes a sword, hidden at the bottom of a cache, the metal cool against her fingertips. A swirl of memories—old scents, old tastes, old feelings, resurrected like blood pressing through stretched-thin cloth. She does not take the weapon. *You will have no need of it.* A voice, near-forgotten, edged in gold and green, whispering within her. Delicious, frightening. Snake-scale-coil in her belly, twist of dread or anticipation.

The travel-pack's mouth closes with a leathery hiss of drawstrings. She hauls it over her arm, weight settling in the crook of her shoulder. Finally she turns, searching. Another cache, unopened. She unlatches it, reaches inside. Rows of wax-stoppered earthen jugs, patinated with age and dust. Inscribed religious text and stylized iconography, pressed into the surfaces while the clay was still wet. Beautiful things. She gathers them into her arms, as many as she can carry, and makes her slow, heavy way up from quiet bowels of the temple.

Returning to the sanctuary, she sets the jugs out next to the rows of bodies, fighting her gorge as the thick stink of death—blessedly absent from the caverns below—pushes at her throat again. The buzzing of wasps and flies gnaws at her from the edges of the room, the distant shriek of vultures circling like deranged spirits. Eaters of the dead.

She cracks the seal on the first jar, heavy scent of spice striking her nostrils. For a moment it covers the smell of gore, washing through her, tugging at memories of this place. Peaceful faces, meals shared and worship given. She walls them away, entombing them until they no longer taste of pain and blood. However long that may be.

She lifts the opened jar, pours the scented oil on the

first body, moving slowly, trailing it in a rich stream over corpse after corpse, watching the liquid pool and darken the shrouding tapestries, molding gently to the forms beneath. Her throat tightens with grief, vision blurring, chin trembling, but she does not stop her work, breaking open jars and pouring until each silent figure is doused. When she reaches her son, laid in the midst of them, she stops, unable to contain the groan that wells from her belly, her womb; deep as the earth, dark as the void that swallows the sun.

Kneeling, she anoints him, oil and salt tears running together over his face, his cheeks, his lips. She gathers him up, rocks him one last time. Kisses him. Lets him go.

Stands with empty arms.

Finished with the bodies, she moves through the rest of the chamber. A full jar dashed upon the altar, running slow and rich down the sides, channeling through age-old carvings. *Let them split and crack apart, let it crumble into shards.* Oil upon the sacred trees lining the alcoved walls, some already charred with the swift-passing fire of the desecrators, thick leaves beginning to wither. *They will burn to ash; let nothing green grow here again.* The last jars for the doorways, dark mouths drinking the horror of this place with traitorous hunger. *Let none ever again cross over your thresholds; you shall hunger forever.*

Her body burns with exertion, the pain of her wounds. Her work is almost finished.

She returns to the bodies, the limp in her step arrowing hot barbs through her heel, her knee, into her hip. Her bones are like lead in her limbs. Forcing herself to look over the covered forms before her, she reaches into her pack, withdraws a small, sharp knife. Lifts it to her head, scrapes it back over her scalp. Clumps of hair patter to the ground, stiff with dried blood.

Head shaved, she replaces the knife. Kneels.

The old words stir in her, latching teeth into things long-buried, drawing them forth. That snake-coil-squirm in her belly again—oiled scales, wriggling tendrils. Shifting, rising.

She lifts her hands before her, palms meeting, brushing softly together. Whispers a word. Feels it spark between her fingers, pale flame on dark skin. Her body thrills. An emerald warmth spreads through her like an indrawn breath, expanding, pressing at the edges of her form. She swallows.

Her hands tremble as she presses them to the oil-drenched edge of a tapestry. The makeshift funeral shroud draws hungrily at the flame, devouring it like a longed-for apotheosis. A final transformation. She lets go and the fire leeches back into her hands, vanishing in a slither of dissipating warmth.

The blaze spreads quickly. A funeral pyre worthy of the god. *No.* Worthy of those who lived and served and died with his name on their lips. More worthy than he would ever be.

She stands unmoving for a time, watching the flames crawl throughout the room, spreading to every surface. They will burn until every stone is splintered char, until nothing remains upon this mountainside but a scorched hollow.

She crouches, scrapes up a handful of ash. Spits into it and mixes it to a paste in her hands, paints the mixture in a thick band across her eyes.

Turning, she moves toward the temple's vaulted archway, teeth set like flint, hitching stride carrying her out into the bright-burning world.

Pale scrub coats the red earth underfoot, spilling over rocky crags, swelling occasionally to thicker growths of short trees and long grasses. Fleshy plants nestle in cracks, fat with hoarded moisture. They crunch beneath her feet, sticky lifeblood glistening in the sun.

She has slept and woken several times since leaving the temple, the chill of night forcing her to shelter where she can: a small hollow, a girthy cradle of tree roots, the burned-out shell of a hovel. With the coming of each night she remembers him, and in her dreams she is naked before the grief, laid bare and fleeing through endless night. She wakes wrung dry, bitter as ash. She keeps no track of the days, pays little heed to the passing landscape of shadowed forests, striated canyons, plains sculpted by wind and sun.

The villages and small settlements she passes as she travels have fared no better than the temple. Smoke drifts from fields of burned crops, bodies wither in the sun, broken houses line the horizon like jagged teeth. War has come. Long-feared, burst forth at last like a pustulant wound. The discontent of kings paid out, as it ever is, upon the innocent in slaughter and rape and fire. The price of pride settled in dead children.

The knot of steel in her chest grows heavier and harder with each scene of carnage, every unanswered injustice. The shifting coils in her belly spread slowly outward, settling back into long-abandoned hollows, slipping through veins thrumming with wakened memory. She feels her body waxing strong with it, wounds healing, joints remembering their youth, pain abating. It sickens and delights her at once, and she forces both feelings down. They are inconsequential. A distraction. She will do what she must with the tools she is given.

A hill rises before her, steepening into cliffsides, trees clinging to shallow cracks with roots like gnarled fists, twisting toward the sun. Standing stones dot the landscape, rippled umber and oxblood, balanced upon improbably slender bases. Behind her, in the distance, smoke writhes lazily upward from the ruins of a small town, the smell barely reaching her here.

She advances up the hill, marveling slightly at the fluid strength of her legs, newly restored. Before her, tucked beneath an overhanging crag like a burr in the flesh of a giant, is a tiny stone-and-clay shack. The door is recessed, built of dark weatherbeaten wood, set next to a round window-hole, an empty socket in a lopsided face. To the left of the building is a small garden—gourds, grain, some hardy fruits.

Trepidation builds in her gut as she approaches the door. Her shoulders tighten. She raises a fist, knocks.

No sound from within.

She waits, sun on her back, sweat crawling beneath her robes. Her stomach churns. The grain of the door's wood seems too close, pores and ridges and splinters all picked out in shimmering, excruciating detail. She raises a hand.

Sudden rasp of a bolt, creak of hinges. The door is pulled inward and she steps back, jaw tightening.

The face before her has changed in the years since she saw it last, but only a little. A few more lines, more grey twining the braided ropes of hair, a weight of weariness held in the eyes and corners of the mouth, but just as rec-ognizable. Just as beautiful.

'Sahada...'

The woman's eyes harden at the sight of her guest, cold as stars.

'Why have you come here?'

'Saha, they have killed him.' Her voice breaks upon the words, the first she has spoken in days. The first time she has allowed herself to say them. Finally giving voice to the loss feels like a betrayal, a last refuge stripped away. She feels her jaw tremble, vision clouding. A stone in her throat.

Unreadable emotions dance for a moment beneath Sahada's face. Then she relents, stepping forward to pull her into an embrace, head against neck, tears on cool skin.

Sahada leads her inside, seats her at the table, places a cup in her hand that she can barely see to drink. The water passes over her lips, silver-cold in her throat. She masters herself, swallowing hard. Looks at Sahada. The woman's eyes are hard as they were before, unsaid words biding time in their depths. Lips tight, jaw clenched. When she speaks, her voice is flat, uninflected.

'They have destroyed the temple.'

She nods in reply, swallowing again.

'None left alive?'

Shake of the head. Blurring eyes, blinked away. A tear cuts her cheek.

Sahada breathes out, long and heavy. Her eyes drift closed for a moment, fingers moving in a small invocation.

A moment. Then:

'I know why you have come.'

Their eyes meet, iron against flint, something nameless twisting in the spark.

'You want to go back to the tree.' A pause. 'You want me to go with you.'

She does not speak. Does not need to.

Sahada leans forward suddenly, eyes flaring, voice hot between her teeth. 'What do you think I owe you? You abandoned *me*. *You* betrayed *me*. After everything, all we faced together, all your pretty words, all your promises. All I gave you. You left me.'

The words are throttled, raw, burning with years of rage and sorrow and hurt.

She cannot answer them.

'So tell me,' Sahada continues, 'what kind of person would return to such a place, with one who has already cast them aside once before?'

Words press at her throat, too large to escape, age-swollen and steeped in a thousand little fears.

Sahada's face closes over once again, eyes cooling to chips of jet. She leans back.

'You never even wanted that child.'

The words strike her like a physical blow, a slap across the cheek.

Sahada blinks but does not look away. Defiance smolders in her eyes.

New words line her tongue like knives, ready to hurl, ready to wound. Shards of a longer self. She breathes in, forces them back, down into her belly. Closes her eyes.

She speaks—low, unsteady with checked emotion.

'You are right. I did not want him.' She pauses around a hitch in her breath, continues. 'He was the seed of a man I did not love, my duty to the temple. Nothing more. I feared him as he grew in me. Feared what I might do to him. And when the time came for his birth I hated him. I hated the pain he caused me, I hated the way he ripped through me and took part of me with him.

'And then they placed him in my arms and for an instant I was sure I would dash him to the floor to be rid of this thing that would chain me to itself, but I did not. I held him. I felt him in my arms, the small weight of him, his hands pushing, his little head turning. His eyes—' Her voice catches again, glass in her throat. 'I loved him, Sahada. I loved him. He needed me and I wanted— I wanted to protect him.'

Her voice snaps on the last word, and her shoulders rock as grief washes through her yet again, black and heavy and endless.

Opening her eyes at last, she sees Sahada watching her still, face unmoved, but eyes glistening with unshed tears. A rush of hope thickens in the back of her throat. She leans forward, voice raw.

'Sahada, forgive me. Please. I need you. We need to go back. Do you think the king and his officials will stop this? Will they bring back my child? They have engineered this as surely as any of those who attacked me in the temple, as any who laid waste to your town. They see only the profit of war. They see land to be gained, glory to be seized, gold for their bursting coffers. We are nothing to the likes of them.'

Sahada laughs, dry and bitter. 'Do not tell me what I already know.'

'You know what must be done.' She feels a red heat tighten in her belly, stirring power coiling around it. 'They must be reckoned with. All of them.'

Sahada is silent, gaze like hot coals upon her skin. Searching. Burning. She glances toward the window, stares for a time. Back to her.

Something turns behind her eyes.

'I do not forgive you. But I will go with you.'

They leave at dawn the next day. The sun's long fingers scrape the sky bloody behind ripples of cloud, skinning the broken land with red-violet light. Smoke still drifts from the town below, thinner now: a haze catching the morning's glow in its net, bruising it ugly. Figures move through the ruins, too small at this vantage for her to tell if they are returning survivors or lingering raiders.

She turns as Sahada emerges from the hut and for a moment the sight of her is enough to snatch her breath away. The woman is cast from age-dark bronze in the day's first light, a war-goddess on the eve of battle, object of fear and worship. Light leather armor wraps her powerful frame, crafted with an artisan's care, stitched with symbols of hawk and bear and jackal—speed, strength, wit. Two gently-curved hilts jut from broad shoulders like folded wings, sungleam slithering across gold-traced dark wood. Lithe power is writ in every line of her, deadly and beautiful.

Exquisite.

Something unearths itself within her at the sight. Awe, desire. Love. She glances away, steadying her breath. Sets her jaw.

Sahada's gaze travels over the distant town, taking in the ruin, the moving forms, her face cut in unreadable lines. Then she turns, striding down the hill. She does not look back.

Few words pass between them as they travel. There is little to be said. They walk from dawn until after dusk, watching the sun sink into the distant mountains, a yolk behind broken teeth. They make no fires and keep to the edges of wilderness, away from towns and cities. Even so, the nights are often haunted by the sounds of ravaging, carried on the wind—clashing metal, shrieking horses; despairing scream and blood-mad battle-cry. The land smells of smoke, the night lit by the distant glow of burning. They listen, unspeaking, each bound in their private solitudes.

As the days pass, the land shifts. Red-painted earth and towering crags give way to green vales carpeted with shrubs and grasses, then to mountain foothills forested in broad-leaved trees, trunks thick and wrapped with vines. The air grows heavier, dense and humid. These are wilder lands, unsettled, rife with legend.

On the sixth day the trees thicken, the forest growing tall and grand as a throneroom about them, the land now turning steadily upward. The ground is soft and sown with boulders—root-wrapped, moss-covered, tall as their shoulders and glistening damp in the dappled light. This is beautiful land, green and whole and nourishing, bearing no mark of men. She breathes deep and feels herself begin to unknot, drinking the rich air, the scent of growing things. A new shoot breaking through hard, wary earth. She glances at Sahada, feels an uncertain smile begin to tug at her lips.

A low whistle. Bark of laughter. Clattering metal and the crunch of heavy-nailed boots as the ambush breaks from cover, sauntering forward, wolves surrounding prey. Proud and golden and burning in shafts of sunlight, all bright armor and barbed smiles. They shout, laugh, tossing words back and forth in their sharp-edged tongue. Leering eyes glint beneath helmet ridges. Their voices thicken, solicitous, the meaning plain behind unfamiliar words. One cups his groin and tugs, smile sickly-white between curtains of lank, oily hair.

Her chest clamps tight, heart beating like a caged creature, thrashing beneath her throat. *Fool. Careless.* She makes fists of her hands, straightens, firms her trembling muscles. Cuts a sidelong glance at Sahada. Her companion's gaze is hooded, tight; languid stance brimming with concealed power.

She feels a thrill rise through her, terror and eagerness entwined.

The group's leader steps forward. A tall man, thin-lipped and hook-nosed, handsome features surrounding eyes like open graves.

His mouth crooks, half-smile tugging at a scar in his cheek. 'What is it you are doing so far from the city? Two sweet mothers such as yourselves?' His accent is thick, twisting the words strangely. 'Don't you know it isn't safe out here?'

Laughter simmers in the air, warm and vile. One man spits to the side. The smell of unwashed bodies rises on a breeze.

The leader pulls off a glove, lifts his naked hand to grip Sahada's chin. Twists.

'Past prime a bit, but we're not picky these days, are we, boys? Still pretty enough.' He casts a look back to his men. 'Let us hope the skin is as smooth everywhere, eh?'

Another leer. More laughter. The circle shifts, closes tighter. Sahada watches the man, contempt heavy in the twist of her lips.

He turns back to her. 'Come now, give us a smi—'

Her motion is almost too quick for the eye to catch. A rasp of metal, blades dancing through dappled sun. The man's arm thumps to the earth. The second blade crunches into his groin an instant later, splitting him to the belly.

She is among them before he hits his knees.

The leader's shriek underlays the sudden clamor, scraping on and on against her ears as he lies quivering on the darkening earth. Sahada is a blur on the edge of her vision, darting and spinning in a red dance as the men set upon her. More screams cut the air. Patter of blood, ringing blade.

She is on the verge of motion when she feels a thick arm wrap suddenly about her neck from behind, a body pressed hot and rigid against her back. Two more of the men close on her from left and right, faces ugly with rage.

She feels her throat begin to close and thrashes, teeth bared, neck straining. Corded muscle beneath her hands, foul wet breath in her ear. The other two reach her as her vision begins to fade, their hands like vises on her body. Panic suffuses her, flashes of memory lancing through the void of her mind. She struggles, lungs burning.

Something writhes in her belly, coiling scale over scale, pressing through her. Tightens in her core, sinking deep. Aligning.

Daughter.

Power like an indrawn breath, dark in her veins.

How I have missed you.

The coils swell. Still.

Flex.

A ripping, cracking, spattering sound, sudden cascade of wet heat, liquid drenching her to the skin. The pressure around her throat vanishes, the weight of bodies along with it. She staggers, vision throbbing back as she stumbles to her knees. The ground is wet-hot-slick beneath her hands.

Her brain at last decodes the evidence of her eyes. A slurry of pulped flesh and shredded skin surrounds her, organs and shards of bone shockingly warm against her palms. The gorge rises thick and fast in her throat. She pulls her hands free, uncovers a piece of jawbone, scraps of gum still clinging to broken teeth. Her belly spasms. She coughs once, spits the sour taste from her mouth. Climbs to her feet. Red drips from her hands, runs hot down her arms, her neck.

The rest of the men are dead or dying, bleeding out their remaining moments in the dirt, kicking, gasping, limbs tangled with wet undergrowth. One crawls on hands and knees, mewling pitifully, blindly seeking escape. Sahada kicks him onto his side. Blades sing in an expert loop. His head rolls free, dark loam clinging to the open eyes and bloody stump.

The group's leader is still moaning, horrible sounds, toes scraping small tracks in the soil. They approach him together, Sahada's measured stride counterpoint to her own wavering steps.

Sahada rolls him over with the toe of her boot. He gasps, shrieks, the sound shuddering down to a moan, then finally a stream of curses forced through bloodied teeth. Sahada watches him, impassive. Lifts a blade for the killing stroke.

She raises a hand, staying Sahada's arm.

'No.'

The word drops nearly unbidden from her lips, heavy as an ingot. She beholds the man below them, scarred skin, cruel hands, blood bubbling from his whimpering mouth.

Memory rushes through her: a soft, delicate body held in trembling arms, bright with wonder and promise; a boy dashing through sanctified halls, all boundless energy and wild laughter; a young man, handsome, kind, shy half-grin lighting a room like the unveiled sun.

Clouded eyes, cold flesh, limp hands lined dark with dried blood. Burned to ash.

She swallows, taste of iron at the back of her throat.

'Let me.'

Sahada steps back, lowering the sword.

The coils writhe within her, desperate now for another release. She takes hold of them, jaw trembling, vision growing crystalline.

The man sneers, opens his mouth for a final defiant word.

She splits him apart.

For an instant his skin expands before tearing in a thousand places. A spray of flesh; bone and viscera ruptured from the inside.

The tide strikes her shins, spatters her already-wet chest, her neck, her arms. Disgust and relish burst within her and run together, thick in her throat, fever-hot in her belly. Her gut cramps, trying to retch again. She swallows, teeth grinding, forcing it back.

For a moment she stares down at the ruin of flesh before her, small tremors shaking her body. Bright, irregular. Almost pleasurable.

She spins on a heel, heading in search of water. The blood soaking her is beginning to dry and curdle, the stink of it pressing at her gorge. Death-blood. Unclean. The ground is soaked with it.

She feels Sahada's gaze upon her back but she does not turn. Will not let her see her eyes.

The cool air of early night covers her skin like a balm, the darkness hiding her, making her edges indistinct. Wind moves gently, inconstant. The trees above are a frail shelter from the void of sky, the cold malevolence of stars. She stares back at them, mind churning, unable to sleep.

'I did not know you had become so strong in the power.'

Sahada's voice is formless and unmoored in the night. The words send a small slither along the core of her, a tiny burble of alarm.

'Even at the height of your skill among the Gifted. I had never seen you... do something like that.'

She is quiet a moment, unwilling to speak.

'They never knew. I did not know. I did not want to be used by them.'

A lull. Leaves rustle, nightbird calls.

'They are dead now.' Sahada's voice again. 'The Order,

the Gifted. The cultists. They Who Remain. All dead or vanished in the years since we left. I have heard reports. Whispers from those who know.'

'*It* is not dead. It cannot die.'

Another pause.

'We do not have to do this.'

The flare of anger she feels at Sahada's words is sourceless, reactive, a flinching away from something too large to examine.

'*You* do not have to.' The words are harsher than she intended.

Soft creak of leather. When Sahada speaks her voice sounds nearer, taut with reined emotion.

'There has never been a place for us. None who accept us as we are. The Order, the temple, kings, cities, neighbors—no one. What debt do we have to them? We could leave, make our own place beyond their reach, live by no laws but our own, no expectations. Live out our days in peace. Together.' The last word seems to scrape her throat.

The net of stars above grows indistinct as tears gather in her eyes, chest tightening to hold back a sob. She cannot trust herself to answer.

The silence stretches, unspoken words tumbling into the rift, old wounds ripping slowly open. She begins to weep, soundless and contained, the way she has since she was a child, body clenched tight against the grief that would shake her apart.

A hand brushes her face, warm in the growing cold of the night, more tender than she could have imagined. More than she deserves. She flinches, a sob breaking free in her throat, loosing the tide.

Strong arms wrap around her, cradling, desperate, a hand stroking her face, wet with tears. Sahada murmurs in her ear, her own voice breaking, the same words over and over.

'Why did you leave? Why did you leave me?'

She curls into herself, guilt scourging through her. The words are an invitation—to explanation, forgiveness, healing. She cannot accept it. Will not. The weight of grace is beyond what she can bear, a mountainside upon her shoulders, waterfall driving her too deep to breathe. She pushes away, still weeping.

Sahada clings tighter for a moment, then releases her, choking back a sob of her own.

She rolls away, body shaking, trying to rein in her crying, pressing it down to the place it deserves to be. Her belly burns, roils. *Why did you leave? Because you are a coward; selfish, cruel, bitter, afraid. The bloody work of atonement is yours alone.* She grits her jaw and squeezes her eyes shut, tears gathering like molten beads.

The quiet grows, spreading slowly between them.

A warm touch between her shoulder blades, brushing the hunched ridge of her spine. Gentle as a breath, no force, no attempt at intrusion.

'I will go where you go.'

The words are raw, bruised, hardly above a whisper, yet bedded in a peace that knots her stomach. Another sob swells in the back of her throat. She swallows it down, hard as a stone. Sinks into herself, unquiet sleep drawing her down with long-fingered hands.

The trees thin as they approach the cult-lands, their forms becoming stunted, half-beautiful, half-hideous. She feels the encroaching nearness as a rising tension throughout her body, clenching her gut, pressing at her temples. Her mouth tastes acrid. The steep, lush-forested hills are behind them and the dry ground now slopes steadily downward, sliding toward a great basin.

They pass crevices in the earth, fetid cavities tucked between shelves of rock and shrouded by sickly vegetation. Dark cracks yawning into darker depths, entrances to hive-like warrens fissured through the earth beneath them. She looks away as they pass by, afraid of what she might see. What she might remember.

The recollections already crowding her mind are more than enough, a nightmare swirl of images she has long tried to bury. Midnight rituals, the earth turning to mud beneath flowing blood and churning feet, frenzied chanting burning in her ears, her throat; great pyres flickering orange over craggy rock and twisting branches, the moon a cracked and yellowed skull above; writhing, impossible forms half-glimpsed through billowing smoke, drifting in cavern depths, passing between needle-sharp stars above; endless hours curled in a honeycomb-cell, drenched in sweat, mind rotating inside itself, visions within visions; litanies of maddened prophecy droning through twisting tunnels; shrieks of pleasure and agony cracking sun-scorched earth; taste of blood and honey on the tongue, pouring over moving lips.

She forces the memories back with clenched teeth and steadying breaths, but they press harder with every step forward—thirsty, questing roots. Sahada is silent beside her, face hard, grim lines about her mouth and eyes. She has memories of her own.

The trees at last give way, and the basin opens up before them, a vast bowl punched in the earth, ridged and riven with crevices, dust snaking the surface on breaths of arid wind. The far edge is almost lost to sight, obscured by haze and distance. A boulder rises from the center, obsidian-black, large as a hill and broader than it is tall.

Atop it, hunched and malignant, sits a tree.

The tree is larger even than she remembers, the trunk nearly as wide as the boulder itself, branches rippling outward from the crown like crooked hands, roots wrapped about the black rock below, worming through crevices, pooling in hollows like spilled intestine. When last she saw it, the tree's base was thicker than fifty men with joined hands could encircle. Distance plays tricks with scale, making it difficult to judge, but it seems to her it has grown even since then, glutted and swollen, roots thicker, branches spread farther.

Her gut rolls at the sight of it, heat licking from belly to neck. Sweat pricks her scalp. A chorus of whispers swells in the back of her mind.

Suppressong a shudder, she glances to her left. Sahada is watching her, eyes quiet. Emotions churn behind that gaze, but she cannot read them. Does not want to.

A hot breeze rolls up from the basin, making her blink. A foul smell, faint but undeniable, something she knows but cannot recall. She grimaces, steeling herself for the first step.

Sahada's eyes sharpen suddenly, tracking the western rim of the basin.

She turns, following her gaze.

A dust cloud upon the distant plain, bright flashes sparking within it. Sun on steel. Her stomach drops, mouth suddenly dry. Looking closer she can see outriders, the horsemen mere specks and thrashing limbs, outstripping the main force and closing swiftly with the edge of the basin.

She looks at Sahada. 'They must not reach it.'

Her companion is silent a moment. Then: 'Can you run?'

Pulse of fear. Resolve like a jagged stone.

With a surge of power she lunges forward, Sahada close behind her, ground-swallowing strides carrying them down the sloping basin wall toward the tree.

Time flows into a stream as they run, becomes the very plain beneath their feet, cracked earth flying away, moments measured in racing steps. To her right, on the edge of her vision, she is aware of the riders drawing ever nearer, pushing her faster. Wind whips her skin and she is overwhelmed with the power of her body, the effortless balance, fluid strength surging through her frame. She exults in it, the feeling edged with fear and lust. Her feet dance against the earth, driving her forward. The sun arcs overhead. The tree looms larger.

She glances left. Sahada is keeping pace but beginning to fall behind, slowed by the weight of her weapons and armor. Her face burns with determination, legs and arms moving in powerful arcs, nostrils flaring with exertion. *She does not have what you have.*

The base of the rock is close, glistening black and iridescent beneath the tree's shadow, waver of heat-haze distorting its edges.

Sudden thunder in the ground, up the soles of her feet. She whips her head around. The riders are closing, swords drawn, horses flecked with lather. A rasp as Sahada draws a sword, not slowing. A few moments more. From the corner of her eye, she sees the distant dust cloud beginning to tower at the edge of the basin.

Her limbs spark with power, coils loosening in her belly as she runs, her course set to collide with the middle of the riders. She flexes, limbering.

They intersect. Coarse cries from the men, ring and flash of blades arcing through air. She ducks, lashes with the power. A rider in the midst of the group jerks, head snapping impossibly back as though caught on invisible wire. He catapults backward off of his horse, wheeling end over end to crash into the earth like a broken doll, dead without a sound.

She hears a yell behind her, whips a look back to see a second man topple from his mount and go spinning to the dust, vanishing beneath the hooves of his fellows, saddle-strap severed by Sahada's blade. Sahada leaps for the vacated horse, her cry cracking the air. Incredibly, she loops an arm over its neck, swings a leg up, and hauls herself onto the beast's rippling back, swaying to match its motion, gathering the reins in one hand.

For a moment time slows. Sahada is a battle-queen riding to war, fierce and proud and terrible, teeth bared, sleek and haughty as a great cat. She rolls with the motion of her mount, braids dancing on the wind. Deadly grace, naked blade. Bright eyes peer down, fix on hers...

She flinches away, almost stumbling. The clash of blades rings in her ears as Sahada trades blows with the riders, grunt and crunching thud as another falls prey, unequal to her sword-craft. She runs on, feeling the power tingling in her fingers, hot in her bones.

The edge of tree-shadow looms suddenly before them, dark and vast upon the ground, spreading like a stain. A threshold.

They reach it, flying across into heavy shade, the sudden cool of it almost shocking. Her belly bursts with power, a sudden renewal, washing like hot blood through her chest, her limbs, the back of her mouth. She gasps, spins, plucks three more bodies from saddles and twists them in the air. Crack of bones, screams cut short. Blood like rain upon the ground. Sahada slashes another across the face, the man lurching back in a stream of gore, his cursing mangled by the ruin of his mouth. She turns away, seeking another.

'Sahada!'

She whips back, almost in time to dodge the flailing swing. Almost. The tip of the blade scores her cheek and neck rather than cutting through them, arcing away in a line of red. She grunts, drags her mount back, rebalances, blade flickering back toward her attacker. Blood sheets down her side, covering her face and neck, spreading on her chest. The blows are savage and unbelievably swift, hammer and ring of tempered metal, both opponents' faces covered in blood and snarling. Finally a feint, flashing loop, backhand swing. The man's head spins away like horrid fruit, a spiral of dark droplets, his body pitching to the ground in its wake.

Sahada turns, catches sight of her, frozen on paralyzed limbs. Her sword arm whips around, pointing toward the tree. 'Go!'

Finding her legs, she turns and runs, Sahada galloping in her wake. A glance over her shoulder. More riders closing. At the far edge of the basin, the first of the foot soldiers are pouring over, sprinting down the slope. She looks ahead again, stomach growing leaden. Sucks a breath through her teeth, redoubles her pace.

The foot of the boulder looms close, black rock stark as a beacon against the bleached-bone white of the earth.

She reaches it. Turns, panting.

Sahada has backtracked, a one-woman line of defense against the pursuers. She gallops cross-wise to them, crumpled forms and reeling horses in her wake, a few unseated riders stumbling to their feet, reaching for spooked mounts. She trades a handful of ringing blows with the last rider, severs his sword-hand with a brutal chop, sends him reeling with a hacking swing through the ribs. Wheels her horse, gallops back toward the tree.

Even at this distance she can see her companion is wearying, her blows heavier, movements slowing. Her shoulders fall and rise in heaving breaths.

She draws up, dismounts. Closes the distance between them with a stride and snatches her by the shoulder.

'You have to go. Now.'

She pushes her toward the slope, urgent.

Fear wells in her throat, racing down her neck. 'No. No, you have to come with me.'

'If I follow you they will be upon us before we make it even to the base of the tree. You have to go alone. I will hold them. Besides,' she pulls at a flap of armor, exposing a deep wound in her ribcage, a sickly yellow glint of bone, 'climbing will prove difficult for me.'

She feels something brittle snap inside her chest at the words. For an instant everything is impossibly clear, impossibly beautiful, stretching out before them in hues of green and gold. Just beyond reach.

Reality lurches back. Her jaw trembles, eyes growing hot. She shakes her head. 'I'm sorry. I'm sorry...'

Sahada presses a hand to her cheek, warm and solid. 'I'm sorry I didn't follow you. Sorry I let you go. Sorry I—'

Her voice breaks. Her eyes are bright, thumb tracing a gentle line against her cheek, tender as it ever was. 'This time I am telling you to go.' Tight, threaded with sorrow, barely above a whisper. A tear cuts a dark track through dust and blood.

She shakes her head again, eyes blurring, unable to form words.

Sahada reaches to cup the back of her neck, pulls her close. Their lips press together, soft, desperate, warm as breath, bruised souls surfacing to brush each others' hurts. She drinks the kiss deep, tastes it with the salt of tears on her tongue. A universe unfolds between them. Fragile, momentary.

She breaks away, heart throbbing like a wound in her chest. Swallows, steadies her breath.

Sahada reaches up, pulls her second sword from its

sheath with a glint and scrape of honed metal. Tears like stars in her eyes.

'Go, my love.'

She turns her back, spinning to face the approaching riders, tall and strong as a sentinel, blades held ready. Then she darts forward, feinting and flowing like a leaf on the wind, spinning amongst them in a deadly, beautiful dance, her grace undimmed by wound or weariness. A thing of wonder, a thing of worship. A final vision.

She lifts a hand, mouth opening, words trapped on her tongue.

Come, daughter.

A sob breaks in her chest.

Your work is yet unfinished.

Eyes hot, vision blurring, she turns away. Begins to climb.

The ascent is dizzying, the stone cool beneath her palms, her body thrumming with resonant energy. After a time of slow half-crawling, seeking footholds as the slope grows steeper, she finds the narrow staircase chiseled into the boulder's face, spiraling up and around it. She follows it, step by step, moving as quickly as she dares, one hand pressed to the rock beside her, fingers dancing over its slick surface.

She forces herself not to look back, not to search, not to hear the sounds of battle, cries of the dying.

You must not look back now.

She finds she cannot look up either, the swaying vastness of the monument she climbs gripping her with instant vertigo, earth and sky shifting out of place, nearly sending her plunging over the lip of the stairs to be split open on the ridges below. Her body propels her upward, ruthless and unflinching, heedless of her fear.

As she climbs she encounters sigils and images carved into the rock, growing more numerous the further she ascends. Familiar forms. She does not touch them. Her mind whirls, feeling overlight and muffled, thoughts clawing through a heady mire. Her mouth tastes sour.

At last the steps reach the top of the boulder, continuing unbroken up and around the tree's massive trunk. She follows them, unable to halt or turn back now even should she wish to. The sigils continue here as well, covering the trunk of the tree, tortuous, interlocking forms carved into the fleshy bark. Beautiful and repulsive. She is high enough now that the air begins to feel thinner, the tree's motion becoming perceptible. From the edge of her eye she sees the army far below, swarming like ants, carapaces glittering in the sun. She shudders.

Finally, she reaches the summit.

The stairs cut inward, rising through the groin of two huge branches, terminating at the edge of a wide, open space. Humped, uneven, formed by the intersection of the tree's spreading crown of limbs, the platform slopes gently downward toward the center, the crux. But at the point where the limbs should converge, there is nothing.

A hole, lightless, yawning, edges rippled and ridged like an open fistula. A throat into the tree's great dark stomach, the ropy bark surrounding it stained black. Profane, grasping halo.

Her stomach feels light, floating weightless within her, bound down by the weight of her body. Sweat spikes her palms. A thrill slips through her, down the back of her throat.

She swallows. Takes an unsteady step down toward the hole, the throbbing void drawing her like a lodestone. Another step, another, balancing on the ridges, moving slowly down to the maw.

She reaches the edge.

Lowers herself inside, dangling from the lip.

The darkness is absolute, a blinding absence, the silence a sudden devourment of air and all the small sounds wrapped up within it. There is no movement here, no breath of wind. The light does not reach even a handspan from the edge of the hole.

Prying one trembling hand loose from its hold, she swings inward, feeling for another grip. A small gasp, belly rolling, and then her fingers catch a tiny crevice. She worms them inside, dispelling the mental image of some segmented thing woken by her touch, swarming over her hand and arm in a cascade of clicking legs. Grits teeth at the fear.

Hand over hand, she makes her slow way inward, skin

crawling as her body dangles over waiting emptiness. The disc of light recedes behind her.

A hollow thump, a flash of pain as one reaching arm at last strikes a vertical surface. Her fingers scrabble over it for a moment before finding a hold. Boots scrape clumsily for a moment, then a toe finds purchase. Grasping tight, she releases her other hand, swings against the wall. Another handhold. She hangs for a time, muscles trembling, ragged breath small in the blackness.

Begins to descend.

Three handholds down, her questing foot strikes a surface, sounding a harsh clatter. Cautious, she tests her weight. The surface gives a little, then holds. She lowers her other foot. Strained snapping, hollow crunch. Her foot drops and one arm flails out, trying to balance. She stumbles to her knees, the ground sliding, crunching, clattering away beneath her. Jagged forms dimple her palms.

She slows, stops, remains frozen as a hollow cacophony echoes through the vast space before finally dying away.

Her eyes are at last able to make out some of their surroundings in the frail light from above. Heat prickles up her neck, a flood of sour bile behind her tongue as certainty takes hold.

Bones. Piled up, layered together, filling the impossible void of the tree's hollow trunk, sloping sharply toward the center. She is perched at the top of a monstrous funnel, its gullet vanishing into blackness.

She closes her eyes. Sweat cools on her flesh, clinging like a second skin. Distant sounds trickle upward, beckoning, almost like voices. Clicking, shuffling, echoing. Dry throats, moist passages like hollow roots. She opens her eyes.

A second light, faint enough almost to be a trick of her eyes, radiating from below. Red. Heavy. Pulling her down. *Deeper.*

She shifts, breath hovering in her throat, and begins to half-slide, half-clamber down toward the glow.

The bones grow darker as she descends, becoming like sediment; solid, age-blackened, fused together. Knots of desiccated flesh stretch over hollowed ribs, broken skulls of men and animals jumbled with shattered long bones, all streaked and stained with unspeakable things, limned in red by the light from below. The funnel rasps and rattles as she makes her way down, body and mind dwarfed by its unthinkable scale. Time accumulates, becomes meaningless, moments clicking away into the endless dark.

The incline grows steadily steeper beneath her, until she is at last climbing down an almost sheer wall of blackened, impacted bone. Her fingers grip whatever small holds they find: shafts, sockets, teeth, their surfaces sticky with age and decay.

A whisper of motion behind her, scuttling click, flash of a moving form from the corner of her eye. She flinches, crying out, feels a narrow grip slip from her fingers, crack of a foothold giving way. Her stomach lurches as she tumbles into space.

Thick, heavy splash, choking stench ramming at her nostrils, her mouth, her gullet. She retches, flounders, stumbles to her feet, sloshing in viscous, calf-high fluid. The stink is that of an abattoir, rotted blood, raw meat. Bodies broken open and spilled forth, poured into an offering-bowl.

Her belly and throat convulse again and she vomits. Sharp scent of bile.

She screams, once, a brutal, animal sound, and feels the violence of it ground her, pushing back a slew of memories threatening to avalanche through her. She spits, straightens, sucks air through her teeth.

The space is a rough, round cavern, low-ceilinged, oppressive. Several fissures in the wall lead out of the chamber, all of them lit with the same heavy crimson glow. The light is brighter here. It reminds her of a hand held before a candle-flame. Fleshy. Organic.

She moves toward one of the openings, feeling the draw of it, allowing herself to respond. The slurry of decay recedes to her ankles, the soles of her feet. She reaches the mouth of the passage, steps inside.

The red glow is omnipresent, growing brighter as she descends through narrow, worming tunnels and intersecting warrens, down chimneys and shafts she has to force herself to enter, barely wide enough to accommodate her body. She crawls on her belly, wriggles through cracks, slithers past dark holes as swiftly as she can, not permitting her mind to wander down them. The air grows thick, moist and warm as breath, rippling with strange sounds— clicking, ticking, shuffling; faint almost-voices, droning and echoing and directionless. Beckoning. Unhuman shapes haunt the edges of her vision, dragging, slinking, scuttling, stalking, always gone before she can make them out, the bloody half-light a pulsing hallucinogen, beating against her eyes.

Squirming through the rippled, throatlike bore of a swiftly-tapering shaft, she feels the passage begin to tilt downward. She twists, gasping, eyes shut, stars forming in the void behind her lids. Feels herself behind to slide, the weight of her body pulling her down.

Thrashing, kicking panic, white and blinding. She is moving too fast, slipping over warm wet stone, plunging into the earth, deeper, deeper, deeper—

Skidding, rolling, sudden loosing of her limbs. She slides to a stop, bruised, gasping, shivering, vision occluded by shimmering red. She slows her breathing, waits for sight to return. The air is humid, warm, almost hot, cloying on her skin.

She rolls to her knees, head still swimming. Blinks, stares. A vast, spherical chamber swells before her, lumpen pillars of stone scattered through it like broken teeth, glistening in the red light. The source of the light draws her gaze, inexorable, inescapable. She feels her belly coil within her, cannot look away.

A glowing, throbbing, cancerous orifice, impossibly huge, set into the far wall of the vault and covered with a veined, bulging membrane. A malign and cosmic womb. Writhing shapes move inside, pressing at the rippled skin, unthinkably immense.

Welcome, daughter.

The voice thrums within her flesh, the bones of her skull, teeth and lips and tongue vibrating with it, warm and cool at once.

How beautiful you are. How strong you have grown.

Molten, lascivious, benevolent. Mother and father and lover and god.

How long I have waited for your return.

She shivers, body answering the voice's stimulation. She opens her mouth and tries to speak, words hoarse, congealed in her throat.

'I... I have come...'

I know why you have come. From birth have I not chosen you? Have I not brought you here of my will and pleasure? Have I not reared you, suckled you, pruned you, guided you? Through all the long and laboring years of your life, back to me at last. You are consecrated to me, fed on sorrow and watered in blood, fashioned for such a purpose as this.

You have grown strong in your gifts, daughter, stronger than the others could have conceived. They are here with us now, in their true and beautiful forms. They have waited for this day. They have ushered you to me, and they shall bear witness.

You have come, daughter, to fulfill your purpose. To birth me into flesh.

Now tell me what you wish of me.

Her mouth moves, soundless, tears spiking her vision. Flesh trembles a resonant song, crawling in her. Desire acidic in her gut.

'Reckoning.'

The word is blood-raw, gnawed edges scraping her throat. She feels the weight of it like lead in her belly, growing hot.

The voice speaks again, deeper somehow, rich as the gulfs between stars.

You delight me, daughter.

A volley of images sear through her brain: the sun burned black, the night sky splitting like a maw, insects swarming over the mountains, the sea siphoned into cracks in the earth. At the cold and utmost rim of heaven, a vast presence stirs to wakefulness, its eye a devouring chasm.

You know what you must do.

From her waistband she withdraws a small, sharp knife—the same she took from the temple they day she burned it down. She stands, drifts toward the red womb on numb legs, kneels again before it. The chamber swells with whispering, chittering, clicking. Dark forms creep nearer. Her cheeks are hot with tears.

She raises the blade, sets it to her neck. Remembers one last time. Draws it across her throat.

It hurts less than she expects. A quick tug, a sting, then the foreign feel of metal sliding through her flesh. The blood wells quickly, filling her throat, her mouth, sheeting down her chest. She coughs once. Through dimming sight, she watches the droplets fall forward, streaming to splash against the womb's hungry skin.

Split.

Burst.

Rolling rush of fluid and flesh.

She is subsumed.

They rise, reborn, new flesh, new being, ripe and swelling with power, limbs and tendrils and eyes and crowns. This rocky chamber is a shell, an egg. They fill it, press against it, break it apart. They crawl and dig and crush through honeycombed rock, shattering, exulting, climbing upward, upward toward the sun and destruction and the new-birthed age.

The crust of earth shatters at a blow from their fist. The core of a dead star tumbles away, the bloated parasite atop it bursting apart in a shower of offering-bones and new meat. They raise their head and roar at the sky. An army of men cry out as one, fleeing before them, rightful terror at their new gods. They laugh, their mouth thick with gore, fear like liquor in their veins.

They lay waste—the armies, the warlords, the towns,

the cities, the palaces and kings and rulers, a trail of ruin, a reckoning, the despoilers despoiled. Not enough. They lope across the land and scream beneath the sun, seeking for what will sate them. They glut themself on destruction and weep that they are not filled. They are empty, forever empty, howling in the night, their arms longing for what they can never hold again.

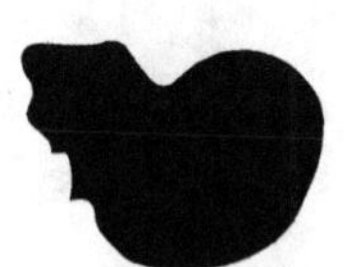

*If you liked this story, please consider reviewing it
on Goodreads or Amazon!*

ABOUT THE AUTHOR

Ethan J. Pollard is a writer and graphic designer living in Oregon with his wife/editor and an assortment of rabbits. He enjoys reading, woodworking, dark coffee, old scotch, the sense of cosmic enormity experienced when staring into the depthless void of the night sky, and the music of Peter Gabriel.

www.ingramcontent.com/pod-product-compliance
Lightning Source LLC
Chambersburg PA
CBHW072138150726

48002CB00004B/1533